W9-DEU-864

How Long Is Forever?

Kelly Carey
Illustrated by Qing Zhuang

Charlesbridge

Library of Congress Cataloging-in-Publication Data
Names: Carey, Kelly, 1968– author. | Zhuang, Qing (Illustrator), Title: How long is forever? / Kelly Carey; illustrated by Qing Zhuang.
Description: Watertown, MA: Charlesbridge, [2020] | Summary: "When Mason complains that his grandmother's pie is taking forever to bake, his grandfather challenges him to explain how long 'forever' really is"—Provided by publisher.
Identifiers: LCCN 2018058509 (print) | LCCN 2019000671 (ebook) | ISBN 9781632898418 (ebook) | ISBN 9781632898425 (ebook pdf) | ISBN 9781580895781 (reinforced for library use)
Subjects: LCSH: Grandparent and child—Juvenile fiction. | Grandfathers—Juvenile fiction. | Time perception—Juvenile fiction. | CYAC: Grandparent and child—Fiction. | Grandfathers—Fiction. | Time—Fiction.
Classification: LCC PZ7.1.C392 (ebook) | LCC PZ7.1.C392 Ho 2020 (print) | DDC 813.6 [E]—dc23
LC record available at https://lccn.loc.gov/2018058509

Published by Charlesbridge
85 Main Street, Watertown, MA, 02472
(617) 926-0329 • www.charlesbridge.com

Printed in China
(hc) 10 9 8 7 6 5 4 3 2 1

Illustrations done in watercolor and colored pencils on 140 lb. cotton cold press watercolor paper
Display type set in Goudy Sans by Bitstream Inc.
Text type set in Adobe Caslon Pro by Adobe Systems Incorporated
Color separations by Colourscan Print Co Pte Ltd, Singapore
Printed by 1010 Printing International Limited in Huizhou, Guangdong, China
Production supervision by Brian G. Walker
Designed by Susan Mallory Sherman and Diane M. Earley

For my mom, who has believed forever; to Paul, who gave me forever; and to Patrick, Jill, and Tim, who are my forever.—K. C.

To Grandma, Mom, and Dad, for your patient support. To David, who bought me blueberry pies for research. Special thanks to Manhattan Country School for inspiring the heart of the art.—Q. Z.

Author's Note

I hope you will discover people and things that you will love forever—as Mason does in the story. Maybe one of them is blueberry pie. Maybe you want blueberry pie right now!

If you don't want to wait forev—umm, a really long time for some blueberry pie, you can visit **www.kcareywrites.com** for links to easy one-minute blueberry-cobbler-in-a-mug recipes. You can read *How Long Is Forever* again while you wait, and dessert will be ready before you finish!

Grandpa's rocker creaked. Mason's foot tapped.
"This is taking forever," Mason whined.

“Do you even know how long forever is?” Grandpa asked.
“Sure,” Mason replied.
“Show me,” said Grandpa.
Mason looked around.

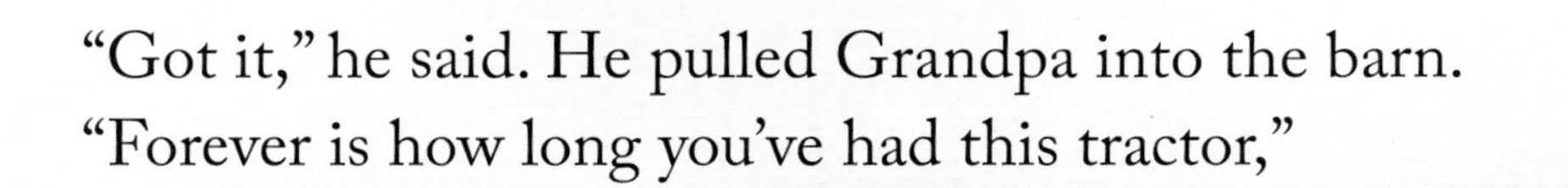

“Got it,” he said. He pulled Grandpa into the barn.

“Forever is how long you’ve had this tractor,” Mason announced.

Springs squeaked when Mason sat on the cracked leather seat. He ran his hand over the prickle of rust on the bumper. It felt as old as forever.

"Not even close." Grandpa laughed.

Mason stood at the barn door.

"Got it," he said. He pushed Grandpa to the chimney that reached above the farmhouse roof.

“Forever is how long it took Nana to grow her roses to the top of the chimney,” Mason said.

He traced the flowers until they disappeared in the sunlight. They towered as tall as forever.

“Nana would be proud that you think her roses are forever,” said Grandpa. “But Nana knows roses are not forever.”

Mason marched down the gravel path and climbed the fence.

"Got it!" he yelled.

"What do you have this time?" asked Grandpa, catching up.

"Forever is how long it takes Mr. Cole to plant his corn." Mason sprinted into the waving cornstalks.

As he disappeared in the shiny leaves, Grandpa and the fence were lost. Mason imagined he was standing in forever.

Then he heard Grandpa chuckle. "Hustle back and try again."

Mason trudged back down the row, took a deep breath, and continued his search.

"Got it," he said. "Forever is how long the water has been racing down the stream."

Mason kicked off his sneakers and let the current dance around his legs. It pulled and swirled as strong as forever.

"You're getting closer," said Grandpa.

He winked and kept wandering down the path.

Like a hint, Grandpa was leaning against the great elm.

"Got it," Mason said. "Forever is how long the great elm tree has been here."

Mason stretched his arms around the trunk. On the other side, Grandpa did the same. Mason smushed his face into the craggy bark and tickled the tips of Grandpa's fingers.

The tree was old and tall, huge and strong. The tree had to be forever.

"When I was your age," Grandpa recalled, "I could reach my arms all the way around. It's grown so much. But even this tree is not forever."

Mason sank into the roots and leaned against the trunk.

They heard Nana calling them. "It's ready!"

Mason raced down the hill, across the stream, past the fence, through the shadow of the rose-covered chimney. Then he bolted by the barn and up the front porch steps.

By the time Grandpa strolled into the kitchen, Mason was scraping the last bite of Nana's blueberry pie off his plate.

"First pie of the season," Nana said. "Was it worth the wait?"

"Uh-huh," Mason mumbled through a mouthful of pie. "Even though it took forev—I mean, even though it was a really long wait."

“Would you like another piece?” Nana asked.
“I could eat a hundred pieces!” bragged Mason.
“That might take forever,” said Nana.

"No," said Mason. "That's not forever."

Grandpa smirked.
Mason shot out of his chair.
“Got it!” he exclaimed.

“Are you sure?” Grandpa asked.

“Forever is how long I will love Nana’s blueberry pie,” Mason declared.

Grandpa nodded.

“And forever is how long I will love you and Nana,” Mason said as he crumpled Nana’s apron with a hug.

“You figured it out,” said Grandpa.

“Did you think it would take me forever?” Mason asked.